WALT DISNEY'S
Winnie-the-Pooh and the Pebble Hunt

GOLDEN PRESS • NEW YORK
Western Publishing Company, Inc. • Racine, Wisconsin

Copyright © 1982 by Walt Disney Productions. All rights reserved. Printed in the U.S.A. by Western Publishing Company, Inc. No part of this book may be reproduced or copied in any form without written permission from the copyright owner. GOLDEN®, A FIRST LITTLE GOLDEN BOOK, and GOLDEN PRESS® are trademarks of Western Publishing Company, Inc. Library of Congress Catalog Card Number: 81-83002   ISBN 0-307-10121-5 / ISBN 0-307-68121-1 (lib. bdg.)   C D E F G H I J

Winnie-the-Pooh and Piglet sat on a log outside Pooh's house.

"We haven't had an adventure in a long time," said Piglet. "Let's go hunting for heffalumps."

"I have a better idea," said Pooh. "Let's hunt for colored pebbles. They're easier to find than heffalumps."

Pooh gave Piglet a big
woolly sock he had found.
"We'll put our pebbles
in this," he said.
And off they went.

Pooh and Piglet hunted everywhere.
Under a tree they found blue pebbles and
gray pebbles. Piglet put them in the sock.

Near a stream they found pink pebbles and yellow pebbles. Piglet put them in the sock.

Behind a bush they found
red pebbles and brown pebbles.

Piglet put them in the sock, too.

The pebble hunters didn't know that there was a little hole in the sock. As the two friends walked along, their pebbles dropped out through the hole.

Into the sock
went the pebbles.
Plunk, plunk, plunk!

And out the toe they fell.
Plop...
plop...
plop...

At last Pooh and Piglet
stopped to rest.
"Let's count our pebbles,"
said Pooh.

Piglet emptied the sock. He counted
very slowly.
Then he said, "One."

Pooh Bear was puzzled.

"Are you sure?" he asked. "Please count them again, Piglet. More slowly this time."

Piglet took a deep breath and counted as slowly as he could.

"One pebble," he said at last. "I counted *very* slowly."

Pooh looked at the sock. "No wonder!" he cried.
"There's a hole in the toe. Our pebbles have
fallen out. We'll have to go back and find them."
"All right," said Piglet. "But which way is back?"

Pooh looked around. "Bother!" he said. "I don't know. We walked too far, Piglet. The pebbles are lost, and so are we."

"Oh, dear," said Piglet. "How will we get home?"

Pooh thought and thought. "Hmm…" he said.
"Ha," he added.

Suddenly he smiled. "We can follow the
pebbles that fell out of the sock!"

Pooh tied a knot in the sock to close up the hole. Then he and Piglet began to follow the line of pebbles back through the forest.

"Here are the brown pebbles and red pebbles," said Pooh.

"Here are the yellow pebbles and pink pebbles!" exclaimed Piglet.

"And here are the gray pebbles and blue pebbles," they both said at once.

Soon the big woolly sock was full, and the
pebble hunters were safe at home.

"Pebble hunting is even more exciting than heffalump hunting!" said Piglet.

"Yes," said Pooh. "But pebble hunting has made me very hungry."

Pooh reached for his honey jar.

"Later we can count our pebbles," he said.

"But first, let's have lunch!"